Sheep graze in fields and on moorland. They grow long woolly coats to keep them warm in winter.

In the early summer the sheep don't need their long coats any more, and the farmer shears the sheep so we can use their wool to keep us warm. The sheep's coats will soon grow long again, ready for the next winter.

A farmer shearing a sheep

At first, the wool from sheep is dirty and oily. Sheep's wool is naturally oily to keep the sheep dry in the rain (the oil helps stop water getting into the wool). So first the wool must be washed to make it clean.

Natural sheep's wool

When it is sheared from the sheep, the wool is the same colour as the sheep it comes from. Sheep can be creamy-coloured, brown or black, or they can be a mixture of these colours.

Wool dyed in different colours

After the wool has been washed to remove the oils and to clean it, we usually dye wool, to make it the colour that we want.

We have to spin the wool, to make it into yarn that we can use for making clothes. Spinning twists the fibres together to make a strong, continuous yarn.

At first people made wool into yarn by using a spindle with a weight on the bottom. The person doing the spinning fanned out a clump of wool in one hand, and spun the spindle with the other hand. Then the wool fibres twisted together to make yarn.

Some people – such as this woman from Peru – still spin wool in this way today.

Then spinning wheels were invented, probably in India. Foot-operated spinning wheels began to be used in Europe in the early 1500s.

To use a spinning wheel, the spinner must first prepare the wool by 'carding' it with wire brushes, to make each fibre lie parallel to the next one – just like brushing your hair.

An old spinning wheel

The wool forms what is called a 'rolag' – a fluffy roll of wool.

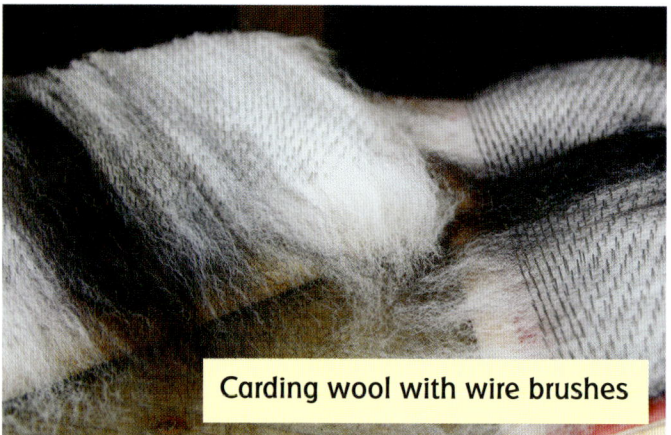

Carding wool with wire brushes

The spinner holds the rolag in one hand and presses the pedal up and down with their foot, so the wheel goes round. The wheel twists the wool fibres into a continuous yarn on a bobbin.

Spinning wheels used to be very important, because people needed them to make warm, woollen clothes. But nowadays wool is nearly always washed, carded, spun and dyed by machine, in factories.

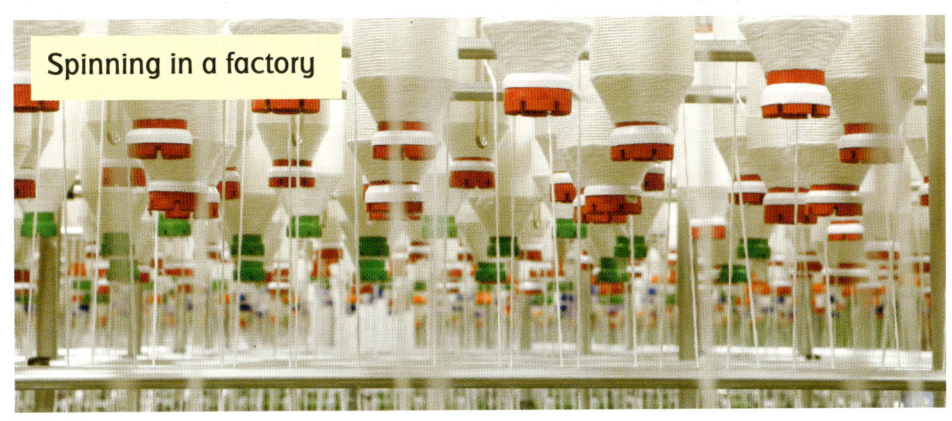

Spinning in a factory

The hair, or wool, of other animals, such as goats and yaks, can also be used to make yarn.

You can mix other sorts of animal hair with sheep's wool to make jumpers. If you have a dog with long hair, you could brush it and spin its hair with wool to make a jumper!

A yak

Shearing a goat for its wool

In factories, different man-made fibres are often spun together, or mixed with wool, to make jumpers with a different look and feel.

For example, the yarn to knit a jumper might be 60% cotton, 30% nylon, and 10% wool.

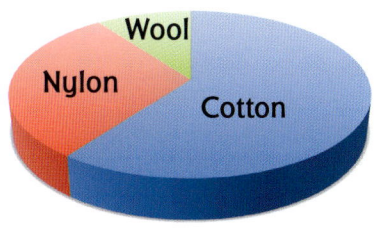

Or it might be 60% wool and 40% acrylic.

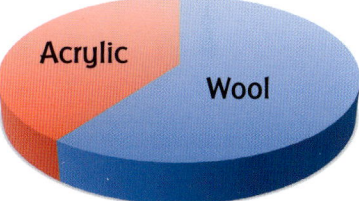

Or it might be 40% cotton, 35% polyester, and 25% wool.

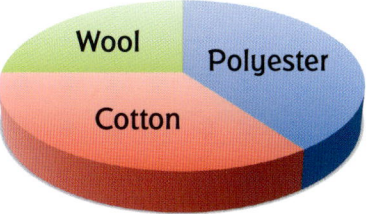

Woolly jumpers are very warm. In 1914 Sir Ernest Shackleton and all his men wore thick woolly jumpers when they were exploring the icy Antarctic!

To make the yarn into jumpers, it has to be knitted.

To knit a jumper by hand all you need are: knitting needles (usually just two), several balls of yarn and a pattern to tell you what to do.

When knitting, each loop is called a stitch. A jumper is knitted by making lots of stitches in lots of rows. When one row is finished, another row is started. The stitches all join together to make the knitted garment stretchy and comfortable to wear.

There are many different sorts of knitting stitches, and each changes how the final jumper feels – for example, super-stretchy, smooth, or bumpy.

Not all jumpers are knitted with two needles. 'Fair Isle' jumpers, for example, can be made on a single bendy circular needle. This kind of jumper is knitted with several different colour balls of wool in complicated designs.

A 'Fair Isle'-style design

Knitting patterns are drawn up by designers. Kaffe Fassett is a famous knitting designer. His jumpers are often made with blocks and stripes of bright wool. The colours are carefully chosen to look good together.

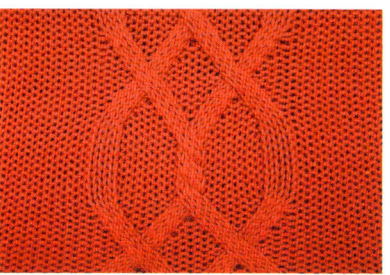

Some people like to knit while they watch television, or if they are a passenger on a long train or car journey. Sometimes you may see a group of people all knitting together, for example in a library.

It used to be common for both men and women to knit.

Shepherds often knitted while they watched their sheep and sailors knitted on board ship, to pass the time. Even pirates knitted!

A shepherd knitting and watching his sheep (1855).

An italian prisoner in the second World War knitting.

A lady called Betty Slinger used to knit while she walked to market. She knitted one man's sock on her way there, and the other sock on her way home!

Nearly all jumpers sold in shops today have been made in factories using large machines.

Before these kinds of jumpers are made, designers first draw designs for jumpers that will look good when they are worn. Then the knitting machines are programmed to make lots of the jumpers. The machines work very fast – much, much faster than knitting by hand.

Because the machines follow a knitting programme, the jumpers that are knitted are all exactly the same. Only the sizes of the jumpers vary.

Jumpers like these are often made in countries where there are many factories. The workers work very hard to make lots of jumpers.

When they are ready, the jumpers are often transported in containers on huge ships. The ships sail to the countries where the jumpers will be sold.

The containers are unloaded, and the jumpers are taken by rail or by road transport to distribution centres.

From there they are sent out to individual shops.

Then, at last, you can go to a shop and buy the jumper that you like. But don't forget the long story of how your jumper was made!